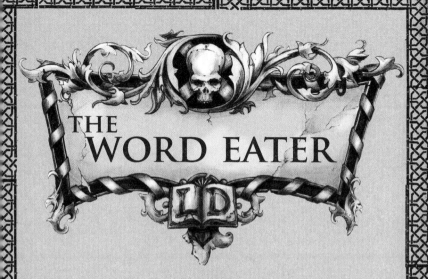

THE WORD EATER

BY MICHAEL DAHL
ILLUSTRATED BY BRADFORD KENDALL

Librarian Reviewer
Laurie K. Holland
Media Specialist (National Board Certified), Edina, MN
MA in Elementary Education, Minnesota State University, Mankato

Reading Consultant
Elizabeth Stedem
Educator/Consultant, Colorado Springs, CO
MA in Elementary Education, University of Denver, CO

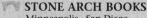 **STONE ARCH BOOKS**
Minneapolis   San Diego

Zone Books are published by Stone Arch Books,
A Capstone Imprint
151 Good Counsel Drive, P.O. Box 669
Mankato, Minnesota 56002
www.capstonepub.com

Copyright © 2008 by Stone Arch Books

Library of Congress Cataloging-in-Publication Data
Dahl, Michael.
     The Word Eater / by Michael Dahl; illustrated by Bradford
Kendall.
     p. cm. — (Zone Books — Library of Doom)
     ISBN 978-1-4342-0491-2 (library binding)
     ISBN 978-1-4342-0551-3 (paperback)
     [1. Books and reading—Fiction. 2. Librarians—Fiction.
3. Fantasy.] I. Kendall, Bradford, ill. II. Title.
PZ7.D15134Wor 2008
[Fic]—dc22   2007032225

Summary: A young man gets a sliver from a strange book. That
night, beneath the glow of a full moon, the man transforms into
the Word Eater. The beast prowls the streets, searching for words
to eat. If the Librarian doesn't stop it, every word and every thing
on earth could disappear.

Creative Director: Heather Kindseth
Senior Designer for Cover and Interior: Kay Fraser
Graphic Designer: Brann Garvey

Printed in the United States of America in Stevens Point, Wisconsin.
092010
005957R

TABLE OF CONTENTS

The Library of Doom is the world's largest collection of strange and dangerous books. The Librarian's duty is to keep the books from falling into the hands of those who would use them for evil purposes.

CHAPTER 1

A SILVER STAB

On a **windy** afternoon, a young man **walks** through a market.

The young man has money in his pocket.

He walks by tables **piled** with old books for sale.

He finds a **strange book** at the **bottom** of one pile.

It has **sharp corners** that are made of silver.

The title of the book is *Full Moon Monster.*

The man **looks up** at the sky.
It is getting darker.

"There will be a **full moon**
tonight," he thinks.

"Ouch!"

One of the book's silver corners has `poked` the man's finger.

He begins to `bleed.`

A small piece of silver is `stuck` in his skin.

CHAPTER 2

A NEW CREATURE

The young man buys the book and then **walks home.**

Soon, he feels **hot** and **sweaty.**

"I must have a **fever**," he thinks.

He stops to rest against a tree in the park.

The moon **shines** brightly
through the waving tree branches.

The young man **falls** to the
ground.

His hair grows into long,
stiff fur.

His fingers become **claws.** His
backbone arches.

The young man has **changed**.

Now, a strange new creature
moves among the trees.

CHAPTER 3

THE MISSING WORDS

The next morning, the young man **wakes** up in his apartment.

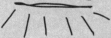

Piles of old books lay around him.

He does not remember how he got home.

He does not know how the books got there, either.

When he opens the books, he sees something **terrifying.**

All the words are missing.

CHAPTER 4

THE WORD EATER

That night, a strange creature **prowls** through the city streets.

The beast **smashes** through the market.

It rips apart the locked bins of books.

The creature grabs a book in its `terrible claws.` Its long, twisting tongue licks the pages.

When it has eaten all the words, the creature `tosses` the book aside.

Then it grabs another book.

The creature stomps by a house with a mailbox in front of it.

It **licks** the name off the mailbox.

Suddenly, everyone in the house **disappears.**

"That's enough!" a strong voice yells.

❰ CHAPTER 5 ❱

THE FACE OFF

A tall, **dark shadow** appears in front of the creature.

It is the Librarian.

"This has gone on long enough," says the man.

"I order you to **return** to your original shape."

23

The creature **snarls** at the Librarian.

It is still hungry.

The creature bends down and begins to **scratch** in the **dirt**.

The creature **spells** words in the dirt.

Then the creature's long tongue
whips out and **licks** at the letters.

The Librarian looks down at his body.

He begins to **fade away.**

The creature **roars** with **laughter.**

Its laughter sounds like books
being **ripped** apart.

The Librarian has almost
completely **vanished.**

Only one of his hands is left.

The Librarian's hand **reaches**
toward the creature.

The hand grabs one of the
creature's fingers.

It is the finger that has a small
piece of silver stuck in it.

Then, the Librarian disappears.

He is gone.

But the creature's finger, with the silver splinter, is also **gone.**

Suddenly, the creature falls to the ground.

Its back grows shorter. Its claws turn into **human hands.**

The man **wonders** how he got there.

Then he hears **voices** and laughter in the dark.

In a house not too far away, people are **appearing** again.

Far away, in the Library of Doom, the **Librarian** appears.

In his hand he holds a **silver splinter.**

A PAGE FROM THE LIBRARY OF DOOM

SHAPE SHIFTERS

Legends and folklore from around the world tell tales of humans who change their shapes. One of the best known shape shifters is the **werewolf** (WAIR-wulf). This is a human who turns into a wolf at night, and then back into a human at daybreak.

The ability to turn into a wolf is called **lycanthropy** (ly-KAN-throp-ee).

You become a werewolf if you are bitten by one. But some people believed that if they wore the skin of a wolf at night, they might be transformed into the beast.

If a werewolf is struck by iron or silver, it will die. And the creature will turn back into a human.

According to legend, the best month for turning into a werewolf is February. The best day is Saturday.

How can you tell if a person is really a werewolf? Look at their left thumb. If the thumbnail is extra long, watch out!

You can cure a werewolf by throwing another wolf skin onto it, but with the hair on the inside.

In countries where there are no wolves, people tell legends about other shape shifters. In China there are were-tigers, in Japan there are were-foxes, in Africa there are were-crocodiles and were-lions.

ABOUT THE AUTHOR

Michael Dahl is the author of more than 100 books for children and young adults. He has twice won the AEP Distinguished Achievement Award for his nonfiction. His Finnegan Zwake mystery series was chosen by the Agatha Awards to be among the five best mystery books for children in 2002 and 2003. He collects books on poison and graveyards, and lives in a haunted house in Minneapolis, Minnesota.

ABOUT THE ILLUSTRATOR

Bradford Kendall has enjoyed drawing for as long as he can remember. As a boy, he loved to read comic books and watch old monster movies. He graduated from the Rhode Island School of Design with a BFA in Illustration. He has owned his own commercial art business since 1983, and lives in Providence, Rhode Island, with his wife, Leigh, and their two children Lily and Stephen. They also have a cat named Hansel and a dog named Gretel.

GLOSSARY

beast (BEEST)—a wild animal or monster

fever (FEE-vur)—a higher than normal body temperature. People often get a fever when they are sick.

market (MAR-kit)—a place where people meet to buy or sell goods

prowls (PROULZ)—to move quietly, like an animal on the hunt

snarl (SNARL)—to show teeth angrily

splinter (SPLIN-tur)—a small, thin piece of wood, metal, or other material that can stick into the skin

terrifying (TER-uh-fye-ing)—extremely frightening or scary

vanish (VAN-ish)—to disappear without warning

DISCUSSION QUESTIONS

1. What's the strangest book you've ever read? Describe the cover of the book and what the book was about.

2. At the end of the story, the young man hears voices. It is the sound of people appearing back in their house. What had happened to them? Why did they reappear?

3. Imagine you could only save one word from the jaws of the Word Eater. What word would it be and why?

WRITING PROMPTS

1. The Librarian stopped the Word Eater, but the *Full Moon Monster* book is still around. Write a story about what will happen to the next person that finds it.

2. Choosing the right words can be the most difficult part of writing. So, have someone do it for you! Ask a friend to make a list of 10 words. Your mission is to write a story using all the words on that list.

3. Describe the strangest item you've ever bought, received, or found. Why was this object so strange? What did it look like? Do you still have it?

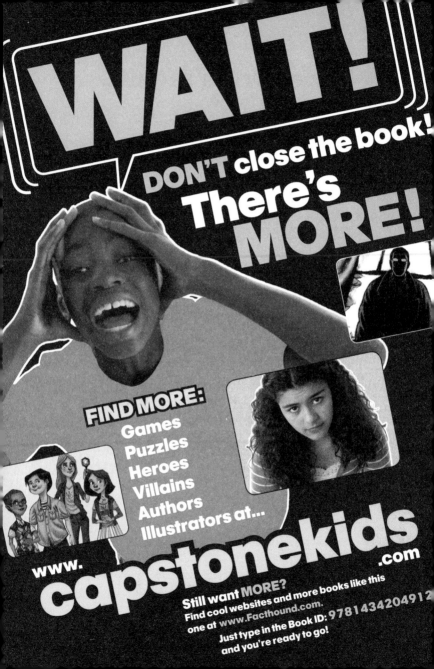